INFINITE DARKNESS

THE RISE OF ANXIETY

MK. AGUER BOL BIOR

Infinite Darkness
Copyright © 2022 by Mk. Aguer Bol Bior

Tellwell Talent
www.tellwell.ca

ISBN
978-0-2288-7246-7 (Hardcover)
978-0-2288-7245-0 (Paperback)
978-0-2288-7247-4 (eBook)

TABLE OF CONTENTS

INFINITE DARKNESS

List of characters, names used, and their English meanings:

Infinite Darkness is the story of Haall, an imaginary African state that just got its independence. Unfortunately, the joy of independence is cut short by a lack of good leadership coupled with social evils such as corruption, nepotism, misuse of power, arbitrary arrests, and assassinations.

Sudd Shujaa *(Brave):* The narrator of the story

H.E.Ms. Melika (*Queen*): Former president of Haall.

H.E. Mr. Maida (*Stomach*): The current president of Haall.

H.E. Mr. Kolera (*Cholera*): Former logistic director, now the vice president.

Mr. Ainu *(See)*: The Minister of Finance, Mr. Maida's cousin, now believed to be an objector.

H.E. Ms. Samaa *(Sky):* The chair of the Trade and Workers' union, and the deputy chair of the anti-corruption committee.

Mr. Mathokraap *(Lazy Person)*: The head of the anti-corruption committee.

Kalaam *(Problem)*: The head of criminal investigation.

Asala *(Python)*: Senior and the deputy of criminal investigation.

Fagaru *(Curse)*: Nephew of H.E. Mr. Maida, police captain officer and Giniita's right-hand man

Shimaal *(North)*: The senior cabinet secretary in the government of Haall.

Cde. Mus *(Razorblade)*: The chief of police in Haall, former lieutenant general in the army.

Dr. Wala *(Light)*: Former president of Belena University, now jobless and a changemaker.

Miss Malaika *(Angel)*: Founder of the Ahsen development program at the university, daughter of Dr. Wala.

Musada (*Assistance*): The president of drama and theatre at the university, now a detainee.

Negiit (*Clever*): The head of the student union, son of Dr. Wala and H.E Ms. Samaa, now a detainee.

Damaana (*Guarantee*): The journalist, host of the *Politically Correct* show.

Amiin (*Honesty*): Wife of Ishaa, an ex-government official, now perceived as a rebel.

Mafi Zol (*Nobody*): Police sergeant, robbery and homicide department, now a changemaker.

Ishaa (*Rumours*): Husband of Amiin, an ex-pastor, now a farmer.

Galtan (*Guilty*): An official in the government, captain with the secret service and in national security.

Azil (*Genuine*): Son of Ishaa and Amiin, university student in his final year, now a detainee.

Nadiif (*Clean*): The most educated professor in Haall, now in exile.

H.E Mr. Raja (*Give Back*): Well-respected politician, assassinated on the campaign trail.

Keniisa (*Church*): friend of Dr. Wala and a former soldier in the army.

Faraasha (*Butterfly*): The daughter of H.E. Ms. Samaa's elder sister, now deceased.

Miskiin (*Calm*): Sister of Faraasha, the daughter of H.E. Ms. Samaa's elder sister, now deceased.

Faka (*Change*): University administrative officer, now an informer for the government of Haall.

Kamil (*Complete*): The founder of the famous radio show *Nothing but the T*, now a detainee.

Blind soldier outside Maida's office, ex-command in the army, now disabled.

Mad old man on the streets of Uptown, ex-policeman, now homeless and on the streets of Uptown.

Shejara Abyei: Ex-official in the government, betrayed by her boss, now has nowhere to go. She has been perceived as an objector to the government.

Bakar (*Expatriate*): Wealthy corrupt businessperson in Haall.

Organizations:

Fok Min (*Above*): The bank that gave a four-billion-dollar
   loan for development, now for official personal use.
Riyha *(Aroma)*: The bank that loaned the government of
   Haall billions of dollars.

Terms:

Keif? (*How are you?*)
Koc aguac. *(Talk you'll get killed.)*
Aseeda: A thick porridge with a gelatin-like consistency
   made from sorghum, wheat, or corn.

Scene One

HARVESTING HOPE IN HAALL

Damaana Newsroom

Haall general election campaigns are hot. After winning the Great War, Haallians are ready for a new start. Women, children, wounded soldiers, and the disabled gather around radios, while others listen from their workplaces. They're all keen to listen to Ms. Melika, who aspires to change the lives of Haallians. At the media house, a journalist asks the aspiring presidential delegate about her plans for the future of Haall. She is accompanied by Mr. Maida, her running mate.

Damaana: Good evening, our beloved viewers. It's such a wonderful night—yet another for our famous show, *Politically Correct.* I'm your host, Damaana, and tonight our guests are Ms. Melika and Mr. Maida, probably the greatest household names in Haall currently. (*He turns toward Ms. Melika and Mr. Maida*) Welcome to the show.

Ms. Melika: (*smiling as her eyes sparkle*) Thank you. It's our pleasure to be here.

Mr. Maida: Thank you very much.

Mr. Maida adjusts his tie and the collar of his shirt, leans forward a little, and then moves into an upright position.

Damaana: (*clearing her throat softly*) Ms. Melika, your political platform objectives state the following, and correct me if I'm wrong: self-reliance, reduced foreign aid, increased regulations in the financial sector, increased funding for renewables, and raising taxes on the wealthy people and corporations in Haall. Could you please elaborate on these items for our viewers?

Ms. Melika: Uh, thank you, Damaana. I want to assure you that the coming period will be payback time for these independence hyenas, if I may call them so, to our people, who have suffered, sacrificed, and even shed blood for the last fifty years of their precious lives in the fight for the independence we're now wasting. Peace is paramount for better living standards for each and every Haallian. I strongly believe that Haallians will judge us by our results. This means we have to show results; we can't and won't betray the trust the people of this great Republic have given us.

Damaana: That's great, Ms. Melika. Where do you aspire to be in five years' time? And what achievements will you have delivered to Haallians?

Ms. Melika: (*placing the tips of her fingers together*) Yesterday I went across Medinna City to inspect the state of our roads, and they don't portray an independent, civilized nation at all. I've held talks with investors and companies in the roads and construction industry. Trust me when I say that the repairs begin on Monday at dawn. *(Ms. Melika looks Damaana directly in the eye.)* By the end of our first term as your leaders, I want Haall to be earning at least 4 billion from gold revenues, 6 billion from horticultural products, and at least 9 billion from manufacturing and other enterprises. So annually we shall have a revenue of at least 24 billion. It's all possible, and to achieve this dream, we need unity and teamwork among all stakeholders in Haall. It's very doable.

Mr. Maida: *(smirking)* In addition, we'll never take Haall back to war. With a thousand tractors, Haall will be a food basket in one year's time; Inu dam will be completed in two years. Haall's parliament will also be ready soon. The airport will be finished before our next martyr celebration. We'll build a pipeline within four months.

Ms. Melika: Medinna downtown will be the most developed place on earth, and the construction of Binia Bridge will start in the next few months. Medinna will be the next hub of investments, development, and technology for the whole region. We have investors ready to build motels, restaurants, and business centres uptown. Haall's economy will be booming.

Damaana: *(lifting her head up a little)* As you both know, we don't have clean water, and infrastructure is a problem. What will your administration do about it? Let's not forget that corruption is a demon in Haall.

Ms. Melika: All areas will have access to clean tap water. We'll eradicate corruption in Haall; trust me, we'll be corruption-free. Zero tolerance for corruption is among our team's core values. All Haallians who have fled the country will return home and make good investments and rebuild the country together. We don't want some Haallians to be second or even third-class citizens here in Haall. Over 20 million trees will be planted in Haall; we want this nation to be a modern, beautiful country.

Damaana: Do you assess Haall to be a success story? If so, why?

Ms. Melika: (*sitting up straighter*) Inmates have the right to educational programs while in prison, and we shall ban solitary confinement, reduce the military budget by 80 per cent, and rebuild Haall infrastructure. We'll increase Haall's science budget and make it illegal for foreign lobbyists to raise money for Haall elections. We'll also implement good domestic policies, raise the minimum wage to three hundred Haallian pounds over five years, and propose a balanced budget amendment. We're going to develop online privacy laws in Haall and make the internet a public utility.

More funding will be allocated to rehabilitation programs and mental health and post-traumatic disorders in Haall. We'll raise the base pay for those in the military service and give reparations to Haall soldiers and wounded heroes. We'll end the wars in Haall and promote peace within and outside Haall. With all this considered, I'd call Haall a success story.

Damaana: Ms. Melika and Mr. Maida, are you sure you'll achieve this, and if yes, how will you do it if you are elected to power?

Ms. Melika and Mr. Maida nod.

Damaana: Ms. Melika, you can go first.

Ms. Melika: First, our team will end the endless wars in Haall to promote peace. Then we'll rebuild our roads and infrastructure and make policies regarding the financial sector.

We'll then start a science academy, harvest all the brainiacs in Haall, and put them in the capital to develop policies. Our goal is to make Haall self-sufficient, self-propelled, and self-reliant in all fields within a decade.

Education will be free for all up to the university level. Healthcare services will be free except for major surgeries or dental issues. Orphans and the elderly will benefit from the monthly provision of basic needs throughout Haall.

Team Melika will hire Haallian intellectuals who are smarter than us, and we'll ask for volunteers as well, especially those who study abroad, to help build a better future for Haall. I know all of you are watching now. Come home, invest, and make our nation great again. We need you.

We'll get every law-enforcer, judge, lawyer, police officer, and attorney, as well as human rights groups, to sit down and rewrite the laws so that we use humane but still strict punishments. We'll ask them for suggestions and criticism. After all, we're doing this for them, so we need them involved as well.

Finally, when everything is in order and running smoothly, with everyone pitching and getting things done, my team will be able to resign, go spend time with family, and give the younger generation a chance to lead us into the future.

Damaana: It sounds like you and your team have the interest of Haallians at heart. But again, like on most occasion, power consumes the souls of leaders, so why do you think you and the whole bureau won't be next?

Ms. Melika: Our purposes, goals, plans, and ambitions all burn in our souls. It's the place where our passionate love lives. If our souls were conquered, then we wouldn't be here today, having achieved so much. And this world is full of setbacks, betrayers, greed, and corruption. It's very important to find your path. *(Ms. Melika looks into the camera.)* And we have chosen to serve you.

Damaana: Awesome! Thank you again to both of you. Are you sure you'll resign after delivering this service to our people? Just asking for the reviewers at home.

Ms. Melika: I can assure you that we have come a long way. The future belongs to our young generation, and we can do our part and give the light to the young ones. It's not that easy, but we have chosen that path for future generations. Our younger generation will ultimately guide Haall. We must always remember that they're the compass, map, and key to our destiny.

Damaana: Wow, that's really amazing. What about the cities of Haall? Does your party have any plans at all?

Ms. Melika: That's a really good question. Leadership is the ultimate vessel that will put Haall's cities on the world map. After assuming office, we'll work on good leadership of the cities.

Personally, I believe putting the right person in charge of the program of any city in Haall is the key to success.

Damaana: The neighbouring countries are taking over the resources of Haall. For example, two weeks ago, the south side of the original Kush was taken. The country is shrinking both from the north and the south. What will your leadership do to make sure it doesn't happen again, Ms. Melika?

Ms. Melika: The map of Haall has been there since long before the Great War, so I shall revisit everything. It's all about foreign policies. Haall's people have a long history. It wouldn't be fair if the neighbouring countries took our land while we were just watching in broad daylight.

Damaana: It's all over the news that your head of defence, Shimaal, has been involved in numerous scandals, such as putting all his family members in the ministry, money laundering, crimes against humanity, embezzlement of the city trust fund, sexual harassment, and death threats against his opponents. Furthermore, the *Haall Standard* published articles about your party and their misuse of power.

Mr. Maida: (*lowering her eyebrows and speaking in broken grammar*) Shimaal is a good son for the soil; he was acquitted by the high court.

Ms. Melika: Damaana, sorry for the interruption, but my partner is right. Here in Haall we have laws and the best judicial system. If Shimaal was acquitted, then that was just propaganda. We owe it to the people of Haall. If the media still has doubts, there is a court of appeal

Damaana: You said this week that when your leadership puts the constitution and the law in order, you'll give the leadership to others. Ms. Melika, I don't intend to be pessimistic, but in case of any change in leadership, are you sure things will happen as planned?

Ms. Melika: Well, we won't be here forever. We just have to do it for the future generations; that's why we won the Great War. We have clear guidance on what to do in each scenario.

Damaana: Miss Melika, I really don't think anybody disagrees with your thoughts. As a youth in Haall, I know that as much as you say you want the best for the future generations, the question is: Is it safe to change leadership here? Can you assure the parents, sons, and daughters of Haall who participated fully in the war? And unfortunately, some lost their lives, some were wounded, and some left with trauma. In addition, a lot of kids were left orphaned. In your position, what will you do for them?

Ms. Melika: We will compensate the families of our lost heroes. As for the victims and persons with disabilities, we'll help them meet their basic needs, and we'll take mental health issues seriously. We have a plan in place for everyone.

Damaana: A quick question: In your own understanding, are foreign aid, loans, and venture capital the best means to develop Haall?

Ms. Melika: That's a good question. You know, any development assistance or aid is beneficial as long as it helps build sustainable internal capacity and is managed properly to address existing gaps. Furthermore, no country in this era can fully develop without external assistance from NGOs, governments, multilaterals, or a combination of these. However, to a certain degree, the government has a vital role to play in the implementation of development. Coupling this with the utilization of resources is another key to development. Haall has been blessed with natural resources. If we use loans and grants, we could reach our potential.

Damaana: Good luck in the coming election. When your team wins, make sure you come to our show once more. Thanks for watching, everyone. Until next time, good night.

The poll and statistics gleaned from the viewers of the *Politically Correct* midnight show indicate that Miss Melika is the right candidate for the presidency. Viewers believe Miss Melika was sent to save Haall and take the country to the highest level of prosperity and development; civilians at the radio station and places of work believed in her. Before the shows ends, the DJ plays "Loachdume." What a lovely night.

Scene Two

FALLING FROM GRACE

Medinna City Stadium, which is filled with Haallians mourning the tragic death of Haall's President, H.E. Ms. Melika. The singer is wearing a black suit and holding the mic as the mourners grieve the sudden death of their short-term president, Her Excellency Ms. Melika, after winning the elections. Some can't believe what just happened. The singer starts singing "Amazing Grace."

The Singer: *(singing)*

Amazing grace, how sweet the sound,

That saved a wretch like me;

I once was lost, but now am found,

Was blind but now I see.

'Twas grace that taught my heart to fear

And grace, my fears relieved.

How precious did that grace appear

The hour I first believed.

Through many dangers, toils, and snares

We have already come;

'Twas grace that brought us safe thus far,

And grace will lead us home.

And grace will lead us home.

The image of Miss Melika appears from the sky, dressed in white with a robe on her waist as the singer leads the crowd.

As the gospel touches the heart of the mourners, this impression creates a sense of togetherness. The people in the crowd hold their hands together and cherish the moment as they believe Her Excellency, the late Miss Melika, is still watching and guiding them from heaven, and as such many might call her our guardian angel.

Mr. Maida starts to read the written eulogy.

Mr. Maida: (*shaking with sobs*) I am honestly not sure. This is ... is ... is a big responsibility that I'm not ready to take. Her Excellency Ms. Melika was a brave leader who stood by the truth and the people of this great nation. (*The people gasp.*) She will be remembered for her role in steering economic development through the different sectors that she supported, which generated a lot of income for this nation. Thank you for being with us today. It's very unfortunate that we lost our president in this tragic accident. May her soul rest in eternal peace.

Before I go further to introduce the life of our late president, Miss Melika, I must share some things about her life. I would say that I'm personally honoured to be in the political bureau. From time to time, she displayed amazing courage, determination, and honesty in the struggle to serve each and every one of us. Miss Melika was known for her bravery, kindness, support, ambassadorial courtesies, and love of all ethnicities, nationalities, and humanity—indeed, for all Haallians. She was a caring, supportive, and loving person. We can definitely learn a lot from her services, both as a civil servant and in a leadership position.

Personally, I think our late president wouldn't want us to mourn her death but to celebrate her life and live in the moment, as we don't know the number of our days. Her outstanding personality and commitment to serving our community still lives through the youth, children, and our leaders. Let's honour her, and may the creator be with her eternally. I urge everyone to put her death behind us and focus on the future, building a life she would be proud of.

As your new leader, and in honour of our late mother, a mentor, I will continue to deliver on the promise we made. As a reminder, this includes but is not limited to:

Total education reform. A proper and good education system is very important for all of us. It facilitates quality learning all through life among people of any age group.

Haall is fortunate to have oil and the most diverse endowments of natural resources. We'll use all of these resources to develop this country.

We'll invest in infrastructure and the road development sector, connecting people from different parts of our county to ensure their participation in all aspects of life, together with the free movement of goods and passengers. Roads are the primary means of transport in Haall.

I strongly believe that industrial development will play a very important role in improving the economic condition of our nation

The tourism industry is important for the benefits it brings as a commercial activity that creates demand and growth for many more industries.

Unity and patriotism are two major benefits of sports. When two people of different cultures and tribes participate in the same game and abide by the same rules, with fairness and equity overseen by a regulatory official, love and harmony prevail among them, and thus the whole nation is united.

Thank you all for coming.

After the mourners go home, the streets and restaurants of Medinna City are empty. You can sense the pain in the hearts and souls of the citizens in the air. There's silence throughout the Republic, and many don't have the energy to go on any further. On the news station and radio, the presenters are trying their level best to play heroic songs in remembrance of Her Excellency, the late Miss. Melika. Although the atmosphere still doesn't feel right, it doesn't change anything.

Scene Three

Three years later, there's nothing to smile about.

Inside Mr. Kolera's office. He's the vice president and is heading a meeting of the finance committee, appointed by Mr. Maida, which also includes Mr. Ainu, the nephew of Mr. Maida, the Minister of Finance.

Mr. Ainu: (*looking up while maintaining eye contact*) Guys, I have great news; we have acquired a four-trillion-dollar loan for the development of Haall infrastructure from Fok Min Bank. This money is meant for Haall's infrastructure: roads and bridges, public housing, and sanitation.

Fagaru: Fellows, this is a lot of money. We have to reward ourselves first before we do anything for the common Haallian.

Kolera: We fought the Great War, now it's our time to eat the fruits of our labour, right? I mean, we fought and won the war without them, especially the young generation.

Fagaru: You said it all. We have to eat first.

Mr. Ainu: (*genuinely*) I don't think that's a good idea. How about implementing Ms. Melika's ideas for Haall? Our party manifesto has the outline we have to follow. Doing a bad job isn't a good idea.

Fagaru: Are you sure about what you're saying? You know, Mr. Ainu, times have changed.

Mr. Ainu: When we took over Haall through the election, the late Cde. Loide said, "If we are not providing basic necessities of life to our people, then the people will drive us into the sea." This was seconded by Cde. Dopure, who said, "Even though there is no sea here, the people will find a sea to drive us into." Never betray the power you have been given.

Kolera: Loide, Maale, Dopure, or Keff aren't here, so we do as we want. First, you weren't here for two weeks. Mr. Maida laid off all those who supported Ms. Melika, so don't be one of them. Even though you're his nephew, you can lose your job too.

Mr. Ainu: We didn't choose ourselves; we were given power by Haallians. We won't be here for life. Remember, Karma has no menu. You just get what you deserve.

Kolera: *Guondo sakit.*

Fagaru: (*laughing*) Heh, heh, heh, *guondo sakit* walai. It's just *kaman*; there's no such thing as Karma here in Haall. It's called survival for the fittest, my brother.

Mr. Ainu: We haven't implemented anything to be so proud of, have we? Where are proper housing, roads, and security? Let's wait and see. Anyway, I can't argue with both of you. We can never sow rice and expect to harvest maize. Where are the president and Asala?

Kolera: Mr. Maida has two urgent meetings today: one at noon with Riyha to smooth everything over before elections next year after we're done with the enemies of progress, and second with Mizaan Bank to get a loan for our trip abroad and allowances. Ahsen Banking also gave us only 200 million dollars last year.

Fagaru: We're waiting for Asala so that we can start the meeting.

Mr. Ainu: (*placing his hand on his cheek, with a furrowed brow*) This is crazy. The government didn't even pay the civil servants of Haall for about a year. Furthermore, the police, soldiers, teachers, traders, virtually everybody are on strike due to low income and the high cost of living. What are we doing, huh? The nation is at a standstill, and our economy is staggering.

Kolera: We're ruling a lot of things out, including the things you just said, but this is the moment to tell you we do not care abo—

Asala, the Minister for Finance, comes into the office, escorted by Hamud, Mr. Maida's security guard.

Fagaru: Ha ha, sir, where have you been? We've waited for you for a very long time.

Asala: (*entering*) Hey, guys, I had to meet this young university graduate. She needs a job, so I had to tell her to bring her papers to my office (*winking*) and see what I could do. So we just came from the Hotel Lusso.

Mr. Ainu: Subhana' Allah!

Kolera: Okay, guys, let's get to work. (*He cleans his left ear with his index finger.*) As you all know, Mr. Maida isn't here. I'm going to chair the meeting. We just got a four-billion-dollar loan from Fok Min Bank. Mr. Maida wants to know your opinion on how to spend the money.

Mr. Ainu: As I said earlier, we have to call budgeting experts, create a budgeting committee, and spend the money as our Manifesto states: transport, housing, healthcare, education, and tourism. In my office, we are behind on the payment of civil servants by about a year-and-a-half, so let's be clear about that as well.

Kolera: Asala, as we agreed earlier, we have to go on a retreat to clear our minds and make informed decisions about Haall's future and our allowances as well. That will cost about 300 million to be exact. We also have to buy new cars for a change.

Mr. Ainu: I don't agree with that. We should call on the experts on roads and bridges—financial experts—I mean, experts in all the fields to help us implement our projects. Arrogance is not a gentleman!

Fagaru: Ainu, even though you're very educated, here in Haall, people don't need that opinion. So shut up!

Mr. Ainu: (*upset*) An ivory tooth is not a cure for a gap.

Kolera: We have concluded. We just have to draft everything, and I'll inform Maida when he comes back. Ainu, you'll get the money for us tomorrow. You're the only one who can read and write, so just draft a proposal that we can show to Mr. Maida on how we've used the trust fund.

Mr. Ainu: But we have to inform Mr. Maida first before I withdraw the money from the bank.

Kolera: No need, it's all good. Just go and do it. He won't mind.

Mr. Ainu: (*holding his head in his hands*) Okay, I'll go now. I have other issues to attend to. The rain doesn't fall on one roof.

Fagaru: We can even use Ainu's signature to withdraw the money and spend it ourselves.

Kolera: Doing this will get him into big trouble, and second of all, this kind of thinking isn't good for the future of Haall.

Fagaru: Just an enemy of progress. Don't mind him; he's gonna meet his Maker.

Asala dozes off in his seat.

Kolera: (*calling*) Asala! Asala! Wake up, man. Did the parliament select you to be their representative in this committee only for you to come and sleep?

Asala: (*sounding confused*) I didn't sleep at home last night. I was having dinner with expatriates. (*Asala sounds more confident.*) They said they were going to give us more money and that they'll take the local Haallians out of business.

Fagaru: That's a really good idea, similar to what we did to the banking and hotel sectors.

Kolera: You know, by doing this we get more resources, and no one will ever compete against us in any way. Talk to Mathokraap; he knows what to do.

Asala: Cde. Mus also will be on board with this idea.

Kolera: This is our idea, so we keep it that way. Knowledge is like a garden: if it isn't cultivated, it can't be harvested.

Fagaru: We don't get a lot of taxes and money from local Haall traders and bank owners, so we should just subrogate them.

Kolera: Guys, thanks for coming. You know this is what we call democracy, where we share ideas and see what we can do with the resources we have. Again, bear in mind that this is a man-eat-man society, so survival for the fittest is nothing personal. We won't be here for eternity, so let's grab what we can and eat as healthy as possible. Mr. Ainu, you raised a lot of good points, but these aren't the major concerns at the moment. We have other work to do ... okay?

You aren't *yesu zadu*, so who are you to judge? (*All laugh out loud.*) Anyway, thank you, everyone, for the job well done. See you soon. Mr. Ainu, for you to keep this job, pick a side. Either you're with us or not. Period.

Mr. Ainu: (*standing up and starting to walk while raising his voice toward Kolera*) So you're threatening me, huh? You know, power comes and goes. You are a fool with no brain, so don't be so bossy. I can't stand this.

Mr. Ainu breaks a couple of water glasses as he speaks. Kolera's bodyguard rushes over and pulls out his gun, aiming at Mr. Ainu with the intent of doing some damage.

Fagaru: Fellows, let's do all this another day, okay? Can we all go home now please? This isn't the right time for this.

Kolera: (*pointing to Mr. Ainu*) I see you, Mr. Ainu. You have the balls to come and intimate me in my own house. How respectful is that? I'll deal with you accordingly. You don't have any respect. I'll show you.

Scene Four

Dancing with the Devil

Mad man short poem on the wall;

Life is never as long as we wish it could be.

Whether you be nineteen or ninety-one or even more,

Appreciate the little things; use your energy right.

Talk to elders and orphans; make their day.

Spend those last few pounds making

a difference in people's lives.

Nourish every moment and make the best of it;

We don't get as many minutes as you may think.

Dr. Wala's house. Ms. Samaa is on the floor.

Dr. Wala: Heyyyy, my love. Hey, please wake up. We need you—our kids, we all need you. Please, please.

H.E. Ms. Samaa doesn't respond.

Dr. Wala: (*calling his daughter*) Malaika! Malaika!

Malaika comes running and starts crying when she sees her mother.

Malaika: Mummy! Mummy, please, what's wrong? Mummy, please wake up.

H.E. Ms. Samaa wakes up, sobbing.

Dr. Wala: You scared us, babe. What happened? You don't look okay. What's up?

Ms. Samaa slumps into the chair. She leans forward, places her head in her hands, and sobs. Huge body-shaking sobs rack Samaa's body, each coming in a wave. With every sob, she lets out a low whimper.

H.E. Ms. Samaa: My sister's daughter just passed away today. I just heard the troublesome news, and I didn't believe it. She just helped me carry water yesterday from the market. What a sad world. Today you're here, and the next second, gone!

A long silence fills the room.

Dr. Wala: I am so, so sorry. Take heart, baby. Remember that God is our refuge and our strength. Keep up the faith. (*He walks over to her and kisses her forehead before hugging her.*) Which daughter passed away? What exactly happened?

H.E Ms. Samaa: Faraasha, the elder one. She was just coming from work and was run over by the police truck at Medinna Avenue. Miskiin took her to two hospitals. Miskiin rocked her sister in her arms tightly, singing and crying softly, which helped her pretend she was just taking a nap. The first one was closed at 2:00 p.m. Upon reaching Medinna Hospital, she had lost a lot of blood, and the heart had monitored its final tune. At the end, there was no point of return (*sobbing*). You know, the hospital has nothing to offer.

Dr. Wala: I am so sorry. I'm lost for words at this sad time. She was a good soul, and for her, I pray for peace and comfort in heaven. In the meantime, you and Malaika will go to comfort your sister's family in this sad moment. We will come later when Negiit comes from school.

H.E Ms. Samaa: It's so sad; we're dead already. This administration is a curse to our souls. If they don't kill us, poverty does every day. If you die of hunger, they will still eat at your funeral. I don't know why we fought the Great War anymore. If Miss Melika and the rest of our fallen heroes of the Great War were to resurrect today, they would be shocked. When she was aspiring to make Haall a good place, death robbed us of our beloved one.

Dr. Wala: Who will implement her great vision? She left us in the hands of corrupt leaders with evil hearts who make suffering worse than it was long before our fathers left for the bush. A sinking vessel has no rudder.

H.E. Ms. Samaa: There is much corruption in Haall. Corruption is just another form of tyranny. We must beware of the people who can do nothing without money, and of those who want to do everything with money.

Dr. Wala: In Haall, diapers and politicians should be changed often, both for the same reasons. It's becoming so bad.

H.E. Ms. Samaa: They always have enthusiastic words, but it's difficult for them to implement those words. Poverty and underdevelopment are siblings in Haall.

Dr. Wala: I know, right? This regime is scared, lives in fear, and continues to oppress Haallians. We shall overcome it one day.

H.E. Ms. Samaa: I heard a plane can take three trips with one propeller. This is rather a witchcraft, not an aircraft.

Dr. Wala: Sacrifices were made during the struggle so that all Haallians may have a better life, but as we speak, some of the people who fought are the ones causing all the suffering of their fellow old-time warriors. We're worse off today than we were yesterday.

H.E. Ms. Samaa: Rain beats the leopard's skin, but it doesn't wash out the spots. People are silent but not calm inside. They shall surely pay soon.

Dr. Wala: First reclaim back our boundaries from our neighbours.

H.E. Ms. Samaa: You're right, Wala, but who is squandering our oil money? Who's benefiting from the trust fund and the loans? We fought to have equal rights, freedoms, distribution of resources, and employment in the national government, but not for this nepotic government. Haven't you heard they took another four-trillion loan?

Dr. Wala: Such an amount of money means making the whole country poorer and poorer. Maybe by the end of two years there will be a billion-pound note. We have so many resources, but our currency is worthless in the international stock exchange.

H.E. Ms. Samaa: Resources don't automatically mean wealth; you have to be able to turn those resources into products to give you wealth. And Haall just hasn't been able to get to that point because of greed, corruption, disorganization, and wickedness.

Dr. Wala: Our soldiers who grew up amid the Great War and oppression might have learned how to make Haall self-sufficient with the resources, but instead they kill their brothers and sisters to feed themselves. What about our leaders? Whatever they do is totally chaotic, that's all.

H.E. Ms. Samaa: We celebrated and congratulated them when they ascended to power, but they went silent after they got to the promised land, leaving us at a crossroads, dying.

Dr. Wala: The solution is simple: give young men leadership, stop corruption, and then use the profits to build refineries, roads, hospitals, and infrastructure. Ooh, but most important of all, we have to pray and ask God for permission—or even wait for him to come down and build us a sample leadership.

H.E. Ms. Samaa: The result of self-hate is wickedness. All they care about are their little families and their greedy circle of friends, whom they wine and dine. Very evil beings in a man-eat-man society.

Dr. Wala: Don't be deceived into thinking that God doesn't have a love for the poor. I think the only thing Haallians know is religion. Instead of tackling the problems, we preach and deceive people. I think it's high time we realized ourselves as Haalians and stopped preaching. It's good to include God in our affairs, but not the way our so-called "men of God" here in Haall do.

H.E Ms. Samaa: Imagine, Mr. Shimaal went to the southerners for treatment for a headache, and they claim to be building our health infrastructure. But because it's not good enough, they travel abroad. If you don't allow your children to eat the food you give to your neighbours' children, then the quality of the food isn't good enough.

Dr. Wala: Total disappointment for our future. As Haallians, we've lost all our constitutional rights to these tyrant leaders. Our judicial system, the military, and the police who took oaths to defend the interests of its people have massively failed us. However, there's something they fail to understand: nothing lasts forever; cards will turn in one way or another.

H.E. Ms. Samaa: Even with such great wealth in Haall, there's still poverty, illiteracy, crime, and poor roads and infrastructure. Our hospitals and network communication are leading from behind, while nepotism is at its best. Is Haallian wealth a blessing or a curse?

Dr. Wala: It's a curse, as the political class is the total authority. They don't care; they're just feeding themselves.

H.E. Ms. Samaa: (*biting her lip*) They just came in without knocking, and they might leave too without saying goodbye. Anyway, even though the eagle flies very high above the clouds, it doesn't reach heaven.

Dr. Wala: (*becoming angry*) It's shameful. How can somebody who has amassed such wealth by denying ordinary people basic necessities come and talk about fairness? Nonsense! Absurd! (*He shakes his head.*)

H.E. Ms. Samaa: Haall officials, like most adults, know the difference between wrong and right, yet they deliberately choose the wrong path. Why? Greed. When delivering speeches at Medinna city hall, they talk about unseen sweet things. (*She speaks sadly.*) What a shame. They can't even lend a hand to the armless war veterans on the streets of Medinna.

Dr. Wala: Haall has always been bedevilled with a lack of knowledge. And worst of all, they refuse to admit that and address it.

Her Excellency Miss Samaa, with her husband, goes outside to get some fresh air. Samaa leans on her husband's shoulder while Dr. Wala tries his level best to sing her favourite song, "Piny a yiin na Akaldu Kaan." From the look on her face you can tell that she loves the song so much that she's willing to put up with her husband's voice. Dr. Wala doesn't know how to control the pitch and tune of the song, and the neighbours were entertained as well for the night.

Scene Five

WICKED HEART, WHERE DID THE ANGELS GO?

Never Lost Hope Student Centre

Wo Ye Tok by Vetino

We struggled, fought, starved and died in numbers.

Together we won the great war; we

were happy and rejoiced.

Every soldier saluted and adored

the remaining veterans.

We buried the falling ones with a smile; we had a land.

Our dream came true, a light at the end of the tunnel;

Welcome to Haall, the Republic of betrayal.

Power chose to divide our very

own sons and daughters;

A Haallian hates her own blood and

is very ashamed of them.

She chooses the expatriates instead of

her mother's son and daughter.

It is embedded in her DNA; her mother's

child is her first enemy.

Telling the truth, honesty and righteousness,

are a way to your maker;

Welcome to Haall, the Republic of betrayal.

The power-hungry deserve a statue

in Medinna City centre;

Unfulfilled dreams of security, roads,

education, and hospitals are overdue.

Love, care, hope, integrity, humility,

kindness, and care are all vices.

Self-hate, tribalism, nepotism, corruption,

misuses of power are daily bread;

Ours are illiteracy, poverty, malnutrition,

insecurity, and darkness.

Welcome to Haall, the Republic of betrayal

Nadiif: Good evening, brothers and sisters. Faka isn't available to make it tonight. The course we're pushing is a heavy one. As we speak tonight, we have to know the magnitude of this. It won't be an easy one.

Azil: We must have a good understanding of the politics of our home and what politics is supposed to produce. If we don't have a clear understanding of who we give our power to, then we be the co-authors of misfortunes.; Furthermore, we'll always be misled, deceived, or misguided and be behind someone who doesn't have our best interest in their heart rather than theirs. So our job here is to re-educate our people and help them think consciously, especially the youth, so that if we vote, we won't bring hyenas into the system rather than people who have our desires at heart.

Nadiif: On the other hand, it's a great idea to own and operate the economy of Haallian, because if we empower one another, then we are economically free.

Azil: We have a lot to do and to discuss tonight, fellows. Most importantly, the things that affect us as the youth of Haall. It hurts me to the core of my being that they don't care about us, so we have to do it our way or never.

Nadiif: Exactly, brothers and sisters. Are we citizens of Haall or not? Look, just last week it was shameful that I lost my cousin Faraasha due to a lack of health facilities. She was a good daughter to my aunt. Miskiin told her she would be fine, and that was the last word she heard. There was only one doctor; the rest were home. In the same hospital, the blood bank closes on Friday, and doctors go on vacation. God, where do we run to?

Azil: I feel your pain. So sorry that you had to go through all this. I knew her because she had the rarest personality of all the people I know. Even though she's gone, she has left a mark in Haall for us to emulate. I remember she had a deep sense of idealism and integrity. Faraasha was a soft-spoken person who strived to do what is right and wanted to help create a place where others do the right. To uplift others and spread compassion was one of her many virtues; we'll greatly miss her.

Musada: I am so ashamed to be the son of this soil. If God wills, then take me with you. Enough of this suffering. My parents died in the Great War for all of us to have a bright future, and now our future has passed. We don't know what tomorrow holds. Every day, we are worse off than we were yesterday. We should greatly examine ourselves. We have turned social media into a tool to destroy ourselves.

Nadiif: It saddens me seeing little homeless orphans on the streets with no food, home, or family. I strongly believe our best days were when we were in our mothers' wombs. Let's go back there to our comfort, eh! And this is what I'm fighting for.

Azil: Hey, brothers, let's all unite and raise our voices as the youth. I've never had a vivid thought of my death or how I'll be remembered. But dying to make a change in Haall is the best way to go. Let's organize a peaceful demonstration before the next election.

Musada: We'll mobilize all sons and daughters of Haall, the homeless, hopeless, and students.

Nadiif: It's now or never. We have the power. If they kill us, we'll all die for a good cause. Even though Mr. Maida isn't bothered because he's well protected, if we die, we'll tell our ancestors that we did our part.

Azil: It won't be a problem if we die, since we're already dead. They'll kill us as they did Jena. A youthful Haallian got killed for no reason, just because of holding a sign saying, "Your Time Is Up" outside the office of the president.

Musada: I'm not afraid of death. This life has killed the youth already—mentally, emotionally, and physically. We're just walking corpses.

Nadiif: They'll probably do what they did at the Medinna junction last year—intimidate us, beat us, and slap our mothers and humiliate them in front of us, just to distract us and change the narrative to the world. What could be possible if you see a helpless mother crying on the roadside, demanding justice for her children.

Azil: Right, the police are always against us. Their mission of service based on preserving the peace, protection of life and property, preventing crime, apprehending offenders, and enforcing the law is long dead. The government doesn't listen to us. They don't care about us, just their stomachs. Empty promises, fake love, neither brotherhood nor sisterhood. Wouldn't it be better if we didn't have the police, or even this government?

There's a long silence in the conference room.

Musada: Maybe things would be normal without this government. This is completely messed up. I believe our politicians are our primary source of cries and sorrows.

Nadiif: Imagine, Jama University has been under construction for twenty years—no tarmac roads in the capital city, only potholes everywhere, full of mice. The proposed stadium is another terrible lie. Our executive members invest in neighbouring countries. We don't have support for the orphans and the disabled who were affected by the Great War, as was promised to us.

Azil: I wish we had a place we could go to and leave our motherland to them. But the question is: Where?

Musada: Listening to Mr. Maida and his colleagues talking about development and economic prosperity is like listening to the devil among the sinners.

Nadiif: What a pity. We were well represented on the Great War front. We paid dearly with bullets and our lives, but now we're paid back with this evil. *(Nadiif becomes angry.)* Is it a curse to be obedient in Haall?

Azil: The leaders betrayed Haallian soldiers after the liberation: no salary, no compensation for the wounded, widows and orphans left with no hope for the future. They also stole the leftovers.

Musada: I still wonder ... the devil has always been portrayed as having no power, yet in Haall he is the most powerful.

Azil: This world will end, Insha Allah. I hope there won't be suffering in the next world.

Musada: For sure. Look how they betrayed our blood sister, Shejara Abyei.

Nadiif: She was always there for us, doing everything in her power. And she got that kind of payback. Left to the vultures. No justice or rule of law at all here in Haall.

Azil: Still praying for justice, liberty, and prosperity in my invalid dreams. There are too many young Haallians dying every day fighting for change.

Musada: It saddens me to witness incidents of harassment, torture, gunning downs, humiliations, and all sorts of kidnappings of your fellow Haallians. It has become a daily dose here. It pains you to the core of your whole being. Where is the love y'all proclaim on your lips? Don't they know that he who thinks that they are standing should be careful not to fall?

Nadiif: Another funny thing about Haall politicians nowadays is that they only care about the meal on the table, and they forget who gave it to them. When you're busy eating, you can't see your back.

Azil: No plan for the next generation; we all face the same consequences. You can have millions, but if you lack vision and an understanding of how things work, you're poor.

Musada: We gonna take our power back.

Azil: The administration is standing up because Haallians are busy sleeping. I wonder whose death or kidnapping will wake them up. Jesus Christ's coming?

Nadiif: Truly, brother, few people control Haall while the rest are sleeping—like a child who wakes up crying for a mother's breast, but the mum is sleeping.

Azil: Haallians are in a great storm of darkness, tears, and pain. Winning the Great War was their only crime.

Musada: I pity the brothers and sisters in uniform. They're fed poorly, if ever, and have nowhere to live. They're impoverished, have no salary, and die angry and hungry. And they are still not on our side.

Nadiif: Look at what the Haall people's defense forces did to our young brother. He is disabled because he was accused of stealing Kolera's cousin's phone, yet it was just misplaced.

Azil: Sadly, civilians are taken to military barracks for trials for any crime. What's the work of the police? Cde. Mus beat a student for looking him in the eye.

Nadiif: Even a single misspelling of a word can ruin your life in Haall, like the tale of a man who wrote to his wife but forgot to put an "e" at the end of the sentence: "I am enjoying myself. I wish you were her." His marriage ended. Not his intention, just like it wasn't the students'.

Musada: People's defense forces could do that kind of thing. The question is: Who are they defending when the innocent are tortured like that?

Azil: Rabuna, please, we're tired of these issues. It's like a lion supervising deer in a plant company. Rabuna, take my life for theirs. We are finished, we are done. *Ku thok jam!*

Nadiif: It was in the *Dawn* magazine last night. The minister who embezzled the Medinna National Museum and the Newside Library at our university has been reappointed as the Minister for Home Affairs, and his deputy is the Minister of Finance.

Musada: We know here in Haall that family planning matters, from uncle to aunt to nephew. It's very usual, no surprises at all. Same all stories ... thief after thief. Who is not corrupt here?

Azil: How did those who embezzled public funds come back to the government? I guess looting public funds with impunity is legal and heavily rewarded here in Haall. I wonder why thieves always find their way back to the table. I guess through the back door. Something must be wrong

Nadiif: Please don't increase my blood pressure. Political breaking news is always on the negative spectrum. It's painful, and nothing is changing.

Musada: Let them eat our public resources. The time has come for them to collapse alone after feeding on disabled, wounded soldiers' money.

Azil: We can even argue that someone must be the mastermind of this puzzle. Could it be the person who appointed them back?

Nadiif: With the total disappearance of integrity and honesty in our affairs, corruption got promoted and became the sole ruler.

Musada: Imagine that they fail in all four tasks they were given. How do you think such people are capable again? The problem is that we, the youth, worship these people, and we sit back and watch them take us back to poverty and dependency. But still we keep them and vote for them and say congratulations on their appointments. It's so sad, *walai.*

Azil: They were investigated and found innocent, so let's give them the benefit of the doubt.

Nadiif: So you're suggesting they deserve the appointment? The head of the investigation was blood-related to them, and the co-chair was a cousin to one of the accusers. What should we say? Congratulations, right?

Azil: Honestly, anything is possible here in Haall. A daylight thief became an overnight cleaner. Rotational grazing in reality. Haallian resources are being raped with impunity, and no one seems to care.

Musada: Ironically, without an uncle or big man to connect you, academic qualifications are useless.

Azil: Unfortunately, in Haall there's no such thing as qualification. You're never qualified for anything. The job market is characterized by who you know, not what you know. Education has lost its meaning here, with no recognition of talents.

Musada: On the streets of Medinna, the voice is loud and clear. We've reached a point of no return. We're dancing with the devil—not in hell, but in our motherland. Maida and his colleagues should remember that the same person who gave them the throne gave me a coconut husk.

Nadiif: The gun you told our fathers and mothers to pick up has become our destruction. An unknown gunman is using it to kill our people everywhere. The suffering is too much to bear; we can't do it on our own. Haallians are sharp, clever people. Having said that, there is some amnesia that enters when we politicize everything. We don't interrogate things.

Azil: Never again must we entrust or trade, our destiny, and the destiny of our children and their children's children to scavengers, vagabonds, and vultures of nepotism, corruption, tribalism, and blackmail who have deliberately backslid Haall's development. The torture of the grave is known only to the dead.

Musada: Truly, a long silence has a loud noise. The Haallians take note of the traitors and vipers that have sold out the soul of our mother. If we were in a just place, it would be called treason, punishable by death. Let the second liberation begin.

Dark Campus. Confused by the Truth.

The lights are off completely. Students don't know what is happening. Were people watching their movements, or was it the usual electricity situation in Haall? They scramble for the solution. Nadiif looks around, shocked to see the lights on in the office of Faka, even though it's on the same power source. They knew something was up.

ACT TWO

Scene One

POINT OF NO RETURN

Daylight Robbery by Junior 10

As Haallians create drama on social media platforms,

Loot nation's resources and deliver

zero services to the citizens,

Importing everything, including culture,

rather than build their own,

Fantasized justices on keyboards remotely,

Create enmity within, no love and care,

Hope is dead, the future gone.

Transparency in our leaders is curious at this juncture;

Ms. Melika was the pacemaker we should all emulate.

Haallians, rise, let's all unite in

love; our future at stake.

Put guns down, pens and papers forward;

Let us build knowledge, schools, varsities, and colleges.

With others, style and everything is

foreign, even the hair and nails;

We suffer because we don't do anything for ourselves.

With no dignity, moral principles, or essential services

The future is ours only if we embrace each other.

But calling our own witches and

demons, there's no hope.

Dr. Wala's home

Keniisa: Hey, Dr. Wala, sorry for the loss. Where is your wife? Let her know we're in this problem together.

Dr. Wala: My brother, thank you. She just left for the market to buy some drinking water; no clean water in this area. She will be back soon. Have a seat, brother.

Keniisa: Thank you.

Dr. Wala: What paper are you carrying?

Keniisa: You won't believe it, but *The Dawn's* headline shows that Mr. Maida has borrowed trillions of dollars from Mizaan Bank for the development of Haall.

Dr. Wala: It's very sad, Keniisa, that these officials have their own class system. They think of themselves as the gods of this great Republic. They like mocking us. Two decades ago, they promised us heaven after the "election," but they delivered hell on earth.

Keniisa: It's very unfortunate; look where we are now. We're at the bottom of the ladder. Where did we go wrong? Sometimes I don't agree with a majority of our people. They think that this government is our saviour. I believe that they are our problem. Death is our saviour, probably.

Dr. Wala: The loans and grants that were given to them before were directed into their pockets. No shame at all. Now there's no food, no water, no jobs, no roads. And they're still borrowing money. How much debt will it take to buy food and water for Haallians?

Keniisa: Truly, I have lost count. Probably we'll be paying even with our ancestors' graves for the debt. It's so huge with no progress.

Dr. Wala: Sadu and Nadiif lost their three children due to the break-in of hungry thieves. Unfortunately, life is like mist or a shadow; it quickly passes by here in Haall. No follow-up, either, as police and other departments are soothing and protecting the corrupt individuals.

Keniisa: Corruption is the new governor in town. Haall is the only place on earth where corrupt individuals deliver press conferences, meetings, and talks on fighting corruption. Every official who stretches a skin on a drum pulls the skin to his or her side.

Dr. Wala: We joke too much here in Haall that even Mr. Mathokraap can establish the anti-corruption committee. And borrowing for politicians is a wedding, forgetting that repaying the debt is mourning.

Keniisa: The Galtan corruption files mysteriously disappeared; some mysterious beings work here, or there's some juju here. Man, the devil is real. And he just got promoted.

Dr. Wala: Haallian politics hasn't heard of corruption since long ago. But now, even the most corrupt still claim to be fighting corruption. Haall is a wondrous place indeed. Imagine Mus and Galtan delivering lectures against corruption.

Keniisa: I do agree with that Karma. When it comes to the money you acquire illegally, the same way you got it is the very same way it will fly away. Turning civilians into something else can't last. You always reap what you sow. Harvesting is around the corner. Time will tell.

Dr. Wala: (*in a reflective voice*) We fought as one and bailed ourselves out as one. Now tribalism has taken roots and has cut our soul deeply. Haallians are so shameless that they lack dignity and pride. The government also uses great propaganda to confuse civilians in order for them to stay in power among divided citizens. It's a shame.

Keniisa: Youths are divided along clan lines. We were once united before independence, fighting for the same course. But now, we're in different dimensions.

Dr. Wala: The other day, the Minister for Roads loaned money for the construction of the proposed superhighway. Instead of being prosecuted for that, they switched them to the Ministry of Finance, on the basis that they were fighting for us.

Keniisa: I strongly believe our politicians are abnormal. Greed is their greatest virtue, but still, I have a feeling they have a high dose of fentanyl instead of the Covid vaccine.

Dr. Wala: This fight will be a tough one to win. Can a man hate what he loves most? The sad thing about Haall's future is that the very people responsible for implementing, designing, approving, and leading the fight against corruption are the same people championing the proliferation of the monster.

Keniisa: I think God has forsaken us. Mr. Maida fails way before the projects start. The rest are deceased when it comes to development.

Dr. Wala: It's ironic that they would sometimes nicely say that this money is for development, but they won't give it to the right people for development.

Keniisa: How can we develop when the Haallian development tenders are awarded to the nephews, sons, and daughters of the politicians who don't have the right degrees and papers but have the right people in power?

Dr. Wala: You know the results. Don't be so hopeful that they're going to make any difference, my friend. You can only hope for their pockets to bulge. No change any time soon. Look, the civil servants eat leaves and wild fruits to survive! What a tragedy.

Keniisa: I always tell my friends that Maida and his group don't campaign to make development; they do it for themselves. You know they control the media so that it airs what benefits them—a lot of propaganda and subversion of reality to the world.

Dr. Wala: Truly, they'll do anything to get to power, even if it means rigging the elections or killing people to stay there for a longer time. And most of all, they'll even fabricate mountains of lies to get to the office.

Keniisa: We have serious retrograde amnesia here in Haall. Total nepotism. No way forward. Look at this: Why would you waste a whole twenty years in power with no development? And we still support them.

Dr. Wala: Hold on a second. These people don't go to work. It's a feeding centre where they don't care about you or anybody. They do it for themselves and their families, yet you still hold your head up and say, "I have uncles in power."

Keniisa: You're right, but still, it's sad that people don't know their rights.

Dr. Wala sips his tea and coughs at the same time.

Keniisa: Are you okay?

Dr. Wala: It's Haall water that is polluted by gases and sewage systems.

Keniisa: (*laughing a little*) You know, Dr. Wala, I wanted to get into Haall politics after the Great War ended, just to make a change in Datian as their governor.

Dr. Wala: (*hesitantly*) Really? I'm glad you didn't. Remember what happened to our friend Raja? (*He pauses for a moment.*) He was assassinated, and the polls showed that he would be the next governor of Datian, but he didn't belong to the political bureau, so he met his Maker.

Keniisa: It was a really sad story; they even killed his whole family. I don't know what happened to the investigation.

Dr. Wala: What do you mean? You know who headed the investigation committee. If you still believe there's justice here, then try it if you want to meet the Maker soon. Politics is dirty here; even the poor are excused from wasting bathing soap.

Keniisa: Hey, what happened to the teaching job at Tosheka University? You were the most qualified individual for the job.

Dr. Wala: The job was given to an expatriate.

Keniisa: Instead of securing jobs for the citizens of his own country, he has resorted to expatriates. No trust at all. Some citizens can't get jobs, and self-hate is at its fittest.

Dr Wala: Yes, *koc aguac*!

Dr. Wala quotes the Bible: "If someone is caught in any wrongdoing, you who are spiritual should restore such a person with a gentle spirit, watching out for yourselves so you also won't be tempted. Carry one another's burdens; in this way, you will fulfill the law of Christ. For if anyone considers himself to be something when he is nothing, he deceives himself. But each person should examine their work, and then he will have a reason for boasting in himself alone, and not in respect to someone else. For each person will have to carry their own load". Galatians 6: (1-5)

Dr. Wala's phone rings loudly

Malaika: (*panicked*) Hello, Dad! (*Malaika's voice quavers.*) Nadiif has been arrested at school for planning to talk to the media about the suffering of students at Medinna University.

Dr. Wala: What? *(Dr. Wala is unable to move or speak for a minute.)* Please calm down. What happened? Where did they take him?

Malaika: *(crying)* They took them to an unknown location. Dad, let's try to go to the police station.

Dr. Wala: Did I just hear you say police station? Please come home right now and see what we can do.

Malaika: *(sobbing)* I'm heading there now.

Keniisa: Is everything okay?

Dr. Wala: Keniisa, it's very unfortunate. My son, Nadiif, has been arrested at school with his friends for planning a protest concerning the suffering of students at Medinna University.

Keniisa: I'm very sorry. It's sad how things are going in this country. Where were they taken? Any idea?

Dr. Wala: I don't have any idea. My daughter wants us to go and report the matter to the police. Keniisa, you know that the police won't do anything.

Keniisa: Dr. Wala, I think your daughter is right. What can we do? That's the only place we can go at the moment, even though the police can't do anything for us.

Dr. Wala: Police terrorism didn't begin today. The police in this place are the problem. They won't do us any good, I know. Also, there's no difference between them and the thieves. What can we do, huh?

Keniisa shrugs.

Dr. Wala: The police have won the trophy for terror, misconduct, frequent dishonesty, and abuse of power here in Haall, which has led to the loss of lives. Do you think we can trust their words?

Keniisa: They have so many problems, but can we do it now?

Dr. Wala: As you say, we have no choice. We have to join these kids. Our time is almost up too, without any changes. We have to fight for their future. There are a lot of problems, not only with the police but with all the branches of our government. They have forgotten our communities.

Keniisa: So we want to join the university student protest?

Dr. Wala: Yes. What are we living for if we can't help the future generation? We served in so many fields in the army and civic life as well. What is our reward? Not even retirement benefits. My wife, as the chair of the Trade and Workers' Union, has been fighting for us all, with no results.

Keniisa: But the risk we are taking is high, so we have to be smart about it. We have to organize the kids well.

Dr. Wala: Exactly.

Malaika enters the house with her eyes swollen. She hugs her dad for a long time, tears falling from her eyes as she breathes heavily. Keniisa joins them and they all start crying. They sit for a few minutes with no words. A room full of silence

Dr. Wala: (*breaking the silence with exasperated signs, pressing his lips together*) Let's go to the police station.

They all stand up.

ACT TWO

Scene Two

THE WHISPERING EXILE

Savage police station near Updown centre

Dr. Wala: (*pointing at Mafi Zol angrily*) Mafi Zol! I know you killed my son. You and all these sinful police will pay for it.

Malaika: (*sighing with exasperation*) My brother and his three friends were kidnapped at school today. We want you to tell us where they are.

Mafi Zol: I don't have any idea what happened. Galtan is the head of the operation; we don't have any power as the police.

Malaika: (*crying*) This is so inhumane. You take people and don't bring them back. What's the problem with you people? The system is so bad! You silence the young generation. Aren't they Haallians too? I hate you. I hope you die. You are cursed.

Cde. Mus: Lady, be quiet. If you continue, I'll arrest you. Period. Remember that this is not your house, so you can tell us nothing.

Dr. Wala: (*shaking with sobs*) You ... you animals! Bring my son back. God will punish you in hell, just remember that.

Cde. Mus: Get out! You're causing trouble. Let me finish with this family.

Keniisa: What? We came to report that my friend's son, Nadiif, and his two friends are missing. Why would you tell us to get out?

Cde. Mus: Are you the father?

Keniisa: No.

Cde. Mus: Are you the brother?

Keniisa: No.

Cde. Mus: Or maybe you are the mother or sister?

Keniisa: No, not at all, but for God's sake, you have to help us with the case.

Cde. Mus: If you're not an immediate relative, then be quiet, or else I'll show you how things are done here.

Dr. Wala: Hey, Officer, what are you going to do? Kill us? You're so entitled that you forget you can lose power, you idiot!

Cde. Mus: What did you just call me, old man? This country belongs to us. One more word and you'll end up in jail.

Malaika: Please, Officer, it's also our right to know where my brother is. He's just a young university student. He's done nothing wrong, unless you tell us.

Cde. Mus: I heard that he was among the kids who wanted to start riots and anarchy in this country. It's a great offence, for your information.

Malaika: (*with determination and while keeping eye contact*) What do you mean by anarchy? The country is on its tipping point with you animals guiding us. It's already anarchy.

Cde. Mus: It's overcrowded here. Let the old man talk to Mafi Zol. You two wait outside; you're giving me a headache.

Dr. Wala: Mafi Zol, I knew your father; he was a good man. But I can see that power has gotten into your head. Watch out ... it consumes people. Don't be like them. Please tell us where my son is.

Mafi Zol: I'm so sorry. I'll write a report and call you when I get any news. For now, calm down. We'll get back to you, I promise. I can write down the report.

Mafi Zol grabs pen and paper.

Mafi Zol: What exactly happened, sir?

Dr. Wala: My son and his friends are missing. They were at school, but I learned from a very close source at the university that they were taken by the criminal investigation department and the police.

Mafi Zol: Okay. Did they cause any violence, or were they in the act of committing some?

Dr. Wala: No. They aren't violent people; they're just university students. There is freedom of expression in our constitution, right? So who is above the constitution?

Mafi Zol: Eeh ... ummm ... Uncle Wala ... How do you know that? I thought you were at home, right? Uncle Wala, we can justify anything at the moment. We don't know what really happened, right? Please give us time for the due process.

Dr. Wala: You talk like you're not from here, sir! A lot of people who go missing here aren't found. So what due process are you talking about? It seems like you people are above the law.

Mafi Zol: (*nodding his head*) Please be calm. Trust me, I'm going to do everything in my power to bring justice.

Dr. Wala: With respect, I can't be calm. How would you feel if someone took your only child? It's not a happy situation.

Mafi Zol: I totally understand your pain, Uncle Wala. We'll do our level best. We don't know what happened yet. Give me your number, and I'll personally come and make things right. I know you don't trust us, but trust me.

Dr. Wala: Okay, thank you.

Wala shakes Mafi Zol's hand while giving him a piece of paper with a number on it.

Dr. Wala: You're a good young man. Don't forget that. Don't let power take your good heart. You're nobody, remember, you're somebody.

Mafi Zol shrugs and looks around without knowing what he's doing. He looks at Dr. Wala before walking away slowly.

Maf Zol visits Shadow Heart Cemetery and remembers the words of his mum and dad on their sickbeds, after a severe lung and liver infection from the waste from petroleum on their ancestral land.

Dad: Son, our life is no more now, but always stand for the truth. The truth will always make you happy ... always. Don't let anything or anybody lead you astray.

Mum: We both love you so much. You have to live and
fight for the next generation so that they won't be
poisoned again.

While at the grave, he has a flashback and sees how
his parents were so nice to both him and his younger
sister, who just was diagnosed with liver cancer from the
same refinery. He is furious and starts crying helplessly.
He felt so close to and proud of his parents, but he didn't
lose sight of his dying sister on her sickbed. He starts
walking and suddenly feels his parents' presence. He
turns, and it appears that he vividly sees them. There
is sadness and trauma on his face, as he's not sure if he
should ask for forgiveness from his parents. Clearly, he
feels he isn't doing the right thing.

He's lonely, miserable, and hopeless as he walks back
to the hospital, thinking of his sister, late parents, uncle
Dr. Wala, and his police service. He needs to figure out
his moral obligations.

Scene Three

THE GOD OF THIEVES, SATAN AMONG THE SINNERS

Wounded Soldier's Wife on the Road

Rabuna, please, we're tired of these issues;

Lion supervising deer in a plant company.

Rabuna, take their life back or mine instead;

We are finished, we are done ... *Ku thok jam*!

Inside Medinna Forest on the banks of the city's river. Galtan, Giniita, Fagaru, and Kalaam are present. Kalaam impatiently opens the car and brings Nadiif, Azil, and Musada out.

Galtan: So you kids are the ones who want to start problems, huh? You thought we wouldn't know about your plot? The government has ears ... Faka, the deputy student, told us. What should we do to these three brats who want to defame Maida before the election and put the press on our necks?

Giniita: (*looking at his colleagues*) In the interest of Haall's peace, we kill them and throw them into the river.

Fagaru: I don't think it's the best way to do this. They're just kids and don't know what they're doing. I suggest we let them go. They are our future leaders.

Giniita: You know they've committed treason against Haall. They wanted to start riots and demonstrations. Our constitution states that anyone who commits treason either spends a lifetime in prison or gets hanged. Since our prisons are full, you can well guess our options.

Fagaru: We've done so many wrongs here in Haall; let's make one right decision. Look, they might have wronged us greatly, but just have some humanity in you, sir.

Galtan: We'll just put them in a self detainment centre until we finish the campaigns for the next election. They'll die of hunger there if we don't kill them now.

Fagaru: Just because you didn't pull the trigger doesn't mean that you're innocent, guys.

Giniita: Galtan, this guy has become a headache for us too. You think you're righteous, and there is a lot of blood on your hands.

Fagaru: I know none of us here is righteous, but why kill them?

Giniita: Because they are elements of destruction to Haall's future.

Fagaru: Really? What do you envision about Haall? At a personal level, I don't think killing unarmed civilians has anything to do with our future.

Giniita: So you're questioning my judgement, yeah?

Galtan: (*in a loud voice*) Heyyy, heyyy, please, both of you, calm down.

Galtan answers his ringing phone.

H.E. Ms. Samaa: *(on the other end of the phone)* Heyy, Galtan, how are you? Three university students are missing at your location, including my son. An eyewitness says the police van took them away. Are you aware of that incident?

Galtan: I'm not aware of anything at the moment, Miss Samaa, but I'll call you back in case of anything. Tell their parents we'll look into the matter, and also kindly send me the name of the witnesses. They could be of great help. Thank you.

H.E. Ms. Samaa: *(shaking her head)* Whenever you get any information, call me. I'll go look elsewhere. Bye.

Galtan: Bye, sir. *(To the others)* We have a problem. There were eyewitnesses at the school when Giniita and Kalaam took the boys. And the anti-corruption lady's son was one of them.

Kalaam: What should we do now?

Galtan: Let's look for the eyewitnesses and clear the mess.

Giniita: What are we waiting for? Let's go.

Fagaru: Come on, guys, we've done enough damage already. Please, let's stop the killings.

Giniita: (*stroking his imaginary beard*) You're not seeing a problem here, huh? We have to clear everything up in the interest of Haall. We can't leave them like this. Let's dispatch these fellows to the Maker. What's the implication if the eyewitness gets to the press before us? None of you is seeing that their time is up (*shaking his head*).

Fagaru: If we do this, where are the future leaders? We won't be here for eternity; our time might be up as well.

Galtan: (*checking his watch*). We have too many problems at once. We won't spend the whole fortune on candy. Let's move on and decide quickly.

Giniita: The threat right now is the devil; we don't have it in hand. But we can come back for these three peasants. We can look them up, and they might tell us more about their whole group.

Fagaru: Okay, I'll take care of the eyewitnesses and these kids. You guys can finish the remaining part of our job.

Giniita: I don't trust you; you're a coward who doesn't follow instructions. Make a slide with mistaken eyewitnesses and you'll pay with your head.

Fagaru: (*talking faster*) Giniita, you caused the accident that took Ms. Melika's life, just because you needed a favour from Mr. Maida. I didn't say anything, since you're my boss. But this isn't good at all. Is it fair to kill the same people we should protect? Where is our consent?

Giniita: Say that one more time and I'm going to shoot you in the head, even though you are Mr. Maida's nephew. Useless!

Galtan: Calm down.

Fagaru: I'm out of here.

Fagaru leaves the scene very upset, shaking a little and very confused.

Fagaru: (*visiting his loved ones and the beloved cemetery*)

Father, forgive me. At least let me say something.

Dad, Mom, I'm very sorry. (*He starts crying.*) I let you down. All I wanted was to serve Haallians, as you both did in life, and to be happy. Power and money blinded me. I betrayed your trust. I have witnessed killings and abuse of power in Haall. I was there when we set their houses on fire. I was there when we burned the government critics alive. I … I was there when my friend wrote a defaming article about my uncle, who went to jail with no trial. I was there when we looted development money. I was there when poor people couldn't get food. I was there. I was there when we created enmity among the people. I was the one who brought fake papers and certificates for them.

I'm the one who is responsible for the withdrawal of money from the bank for Giniita and throwing away bodies at night—bodies of those killed "in the interest of peace." I'm very, very sorry. We misuse police authority to serve the leaders. I don't want to be a puppet to this system anymore.

I love you, Dad, Mom. See you soon.

Fagaru shoots himself. His body slides into the tall grass over his father's grave.

ACT TWO

Scene Four

THE QUEEN OF IRON AND WATER

At a famous Radio show, <u>Nothing but the T</u>.

Radio Presenter One: Government beating of youth and three missing university students among others has sparked swift and angry responses from the citizens across Haall. This morning our "hot topic question" is: Can we consider Haall as a great country?

Response One: A great country contains values, virtues, laws, good leadership, and equality. Leaders who listen and sacrifice for their people. What does Haall have, insomnia?

Response Two: Being great means not leaving nobody out, so taking care of orphans, widows, and poor citizens. Have we ever seen our leaders doing this? No. The only great country is Great Sahara; the clue is just in the names.

Radio Presenter Two: It's expected that citizens might go on the streets to protest.

Mr. Maida's office, the greedy heaven

Blind Soldier outside Maida's Office: (*crying*) We're going to leave someday. What have we done to deserve this suffering? After the Great War, we thought everything would be great. We'll have hospitals, roads, good schools, lights, and electricity. Here we are today, worse than before the Great War. The Maida administration has failed us. We only drink clean water in our nightmares. Families are dying of hunger.

Homelessness and hopelessness are the order of the day. Are we not human enough? We deserve better. If our ancestors can hear me now, I hope they change the situation. It's going to change, but God too has forsaken Haall. We are on our own now. We've been praying and fasting for our people, but it seems there is no God anymore. Please, please, by the blood of my ancestors, hear my cry.

Cde. Mus: (*clearing his throat*) Your Excellency, things are getting out of hand now in Haall. University students have caused great havoc here; they've infiltrated the heart and soul of many, even among us.

Mr. Maida: (*freezes and stares with wide eyes and raised eyebrows*) What? We have to do something about this right now.

Cde. Mus: We'll hold a press conference in your office tomorrow, just before the new election after the constitution change. We must keep calm and look like everything is normal. As the police, nationality is always on our side. We'll eliminate those who think they can overthrow us, especially these small university kids and netizens. They've entered social media, so we have to shut down the internet as quickly as possible.

Mr. Maida: (*straddling the chair*) That's amazing to hear. You have to do something right now. We have to meet at my office here tomorrow before things get out of hand, okay?

Samaa, the chair of Trade and Workers' Union, and the deputy chair of the anti-corruption committee, rushes into the office. The police try to stop her from interrupting the meeting.

H.E. Ms. Samaa: Hey, sir, what have we done to deserve this kind of treatment? You said in your speech last time that Haall was liberated for good. Where is my son?

Cde. Mus: Sir, should I take care of her? She shouldn't be here.

Mr. Maida: No, leave her. This is the result of you and your colleagues not taking care of the job properly.

Cde. Mus: But, sir—

Mr. Maida: No, it's all good. (*He turns to Samaa.*) You know I'm glad to see you with this kind of courage to face the issue, especially after all the nonsense your son posted on social media and what he started at the university. It's a risk you took to come here. You are of a low class, so we cannot sit at the same table.

H.E Ms. Samaa: (*swallowing hard*) What brought me here is my son and his friends, as a mother not as a minister. The police took them to an unknown location. They did nothing wrong other than telling the truth about your failures. Since you ascended to power, nothing has been achieved. There's nothing to be proud of, honestly.

Mr. Maida: (*crinkling his eyes and nose*) I've heard about your son and his friends. Ask the police. First, I'm not the police. I am the president. Second, are you blind? You don't see the roads near my home and my ministers' homes? What else do you want … lemonade?

H.E. Ms. Samaa: The police work for you, so you have to know. Otherwise, it wouldn't end well. So you are proud of just this road between your homes? How about Haallians? Where are hospitals, schools, electricity, water?

Mr. Maida: Lady, we fought the war and won, so you can't intimidate me ... okay? It's time we reward ourselves. Let's finish eating; your time is gonna come, don't worry.

H.E. Ms. Samaa: (*almost to herself*) I think I'm legally blind. Pastor Gatluak says the world will end the next day. I will keep everything to myself for the sake of my children, even though the world never ends. We have no love. We have raw materials but die of hunger. Bad leaders. What an irony. Anyway, why sell raw materials for fifteen years, huh? No industries at all, or even one at least. How much does it cost to add value to it? Who bewitched Haallians?

Mr. Maida: Lady, you think we politicians are the problem in Haall? Let me tell you something—I'm the one at work here, yet you accuse me of embezzling funds, this and that. Let's be honest. What have you done for this country? How is the corruption going since you're the chair, huh? The Trade and Workers' Union isn't going well either, and you're in my office, so talk to me nicely. (*He giggles.*)

H.E. Ms. Samaa: (*unblinking*) You have been the head of Haall for twelve good years. You should be raising the minimum wage for civil servants instead of everyone fending for themselves. Don't talk about corruption—you're one of them, with billions of dollars missing. Tell me, where are the trillion dollars you borrowed? Where are the things you said? And you wanted to be elected again. Are you not ashamed of yourself? Where did your moral standing go? Your nephew is the head of finance, the chairman is your in-law, and the secretary to the anti-corruption committee is your son. How can I fight your family, huh? Tell me, Mr. President, how many people have you lifted out of poverty? How can you stand for vegetarianism when you're enjoying that steak?

Mr. Maida: (*proudly*) Stop criticizing the government when you haven't been supporting us through all these years with your Workers' Union. Where were you all when I and my comrades were fighting for your freedom? All these false allegations against me and my friends are void because there is no evidence.

My family is my family, so keep your failure to yourself.

H.E. Ms. Samaa: Do not pretend to be a white fowl.

Mr. Maida: It's easy for you women to have the audacity to look into my eye—I, Mr. Maida, your president—and talk to me like that, saying I'm a tribal, corrupt, and greedy person.

H.E. Ms. Samaa: It's depressing when you try to twist the narrative from the real issue, sir. Your collective amnesia is what baffles me. Haall is sinking on so many fronts: economically, loan borrowing, and corruption. Stop romanticizing corruption. We either work with what is already borrowed or recover the stolen trust fund. It's that simple.

Mr. Maida: (*slamming his fist on the table*) Tell me, who is to blame for all the miseries of Haall? And all this division along tribal lines? Is it not the Haallians themselves? (*He gets pumped up.*) I am what Haall deserves, since I fought for it.

H.E. Ms. Samaa: (*calmly*) While you're inside the driver's seat, you see the road differently. For now, keep praising the sidewalks. Your services barely meet the basic minimum needs of Haallians. You're just in your comfort zone, Mr. President.

Mr. Maida: Speak no ill of midwives while childbirth continues.

H.E. Ms. Samaa: If the Haall political bureau has jailed or unearthed the corrupt officials and politicians' aides, we could soberly discuss this topic. For now, development is just another joke on your lips, sir.

Mr. Maida: Tell me of one corrupt official in my administration.

With mouth agape, Miss Samaa leans her head forward.

H.E. Ms. Samaa: Just in case, ask your Minister of Roads. How many kilometres of road is tarmac in Medinna City? How many feeder roads and bridges have been built in your time? Where did all the trillions of borrowed pounds go? Do you know the living standards of Haallians? How many universities, training centres, high schools have you created?

How many referral hospitals are working, and what is our healthcare system, if we have one?

What is our foreign policy on trade and imports? How many stadiums and sporting activities do Haallians get involved with? What's our country's vision for the next decade? How many jobs have you created for the youth? Do you have any plans for the future of Haall?

Mr. Maida: (*rests his chin on his hand while leaning back and looking up*) Look at the beautiful roads in front of my house. And by the way, a big mall is coming up soon, and a high-level hospital too. And when the election comes, I'll just give Aseeda, the electoral chairman, some pounds. I won't beg him to take it. Now you're still blaming me? So you're gonna blame me for the drought and famine too?

H.E. Ms. Samaa: (*shrugging while shaking her head*) The hypocrisy and ignorance in you and your colleagues are on another level, driven by greed that does not bring forth any good but just misfortunes.

Mr. Maida: Lady, you have no say here in my cabinet. We are the executive members, not civil servants, okay? If you make a joke out of the process, it doesn't work very well.

H.E. Ms. Samaa: You jailed innocent people and killed your opponent. What kind of person are you? Your judicial system is another big mess with so many layers of issues: wrongful detention, misuse of power, and most of all, the negligence in this department.

Mr. Maida: This is politics, lady. If a fool becomes enlightened, a wise man like me is in trouble. I can't let Haallians know the ways of politics.

H.E. Ms. Samaa: Two days ago, Mama Cee lost her only daughter due to the lack of blood in a major hospital here in Haall. Mr. Civilian lost both his beloved wife and unborn child at the hospital due to complications, and a granny got injected with the wrong drug and died. What kind of government have we? (*She crosses her arms.*) Do we even have a health policy?

Mr. Maida: (*shrugging one shoulder*) We're sorry that happened, but it's only one incident. How much good have we done for Haall?

H.E. Ms. Samaa: Mention one good thing your administration has done to help Haallians, in any sector, from finance to the Ministry of Labour, public services, or human resource development.

Mr. Maida: Listen, lady, we've done so much. (*He shifts his eyes back and forth.*) If I were to put it down on paper, it would fill the books in the university library. You people don't value your leader.

H.E. Ms. Samaa: (*with a tight-lipped smile*) I only know about corruption, tribalism, and nepotism, besides the money you've stolen and the property you own abroad, bought with our money.

Mr. Maida: Look, lady, how am I corrupt, huh?

H.E. Ms. Samaa: Our only curse is our good hearts; we forgive and forget easily. If not for that, we wouldn't even allow some individuals like you to be leaders. We're only here because we sold our votes for the money you stole. Shame on us all. Just a reminder, sir ... corruption is your greed, my president. It will never fill your need. Trust me, I can guarantee that.

Mr. Maida: (*pounding a fist on the table while talking*) You've interrupted enough. Get out of my house now!

H.E. Ms. Samaa: Your time is coming.

Ms. Samaa leaves the office.

Mr. Maida: Hey, lady, I'll around for the sequel.

Mr. Maida wanders in his office, peeks out the window, and then sits down for a second. He then takes a long drink of water. He looks at his eulogy of Miss Melika at the wall. He tries calling his wife, but she doesn't pick up. He sits silently holding his phone.

Scene Five

DAYLIGHT BETRAYAL

Mr. Maida's office, the greedy heaven

Morning thought:

A husband goes to the bank to get a home loan and names his wife as guarantor. Unfortunately, the husband decides to channel the money to alcohol and gambling until there's no money left.

He comes back drunk, bragging that he is the man of the house, and states that he can do what he wants, scaring his wife so that she doesn't question how he spent the money. What do you think will happen next?

Mr. Maida: (*coming out of his office*) What's going on here?

Cde. Mus: Things are tough now. Fagaru killed himself, and people are rioting because of the missing kids.

Giniita: I don't know what to do. We have to do something, especially for the very angry university students.

Mr. Maida: I am the president and I'll do as I wish. Send out the police and the anti-riot squad.

Giniita: I don't think that's a good idea. I heard word on the streets that we're not good enough, and we now have cancer in Haall. I'm so shocked to hear about the swelling headed by Mr. Ainu, Maf Zol, Dr. Wala. H.E. Ms. Samaa, Keniisa, university students, and netizens, among others.

Mr. Maida: What? Mr. Ainu, you can feel a stray dog here. I knew about the Trade and Workers' Union; she's a little bit hot-headed. We have to immolate them immediately. Call the rest of my team.

Cde. Mus: Kill them if we have to. Where are the rest of the team members, Giniita?

Ginita: I don't know. Shimal, the Minister of Defence, isn't here. We can also bribe them. You know, with this poverty in Haall, there's a chance we can get away with anything.

Mr. Maida: Yes, at this point we have to campaign for ourselves, make us their favourites. We'll give them some money to silence them. A lot of them are very poor, so they'll keep quiet just at the sight of a note in their palms.

Giniita: Sir, you can talk on national television and calm them, say you heard what they're saying and promise them a better tomorrow.

Cde. Mus: That's great. We'll organize that for you. Talk about a few things here and there. We'll write your speech.

Mr. Maida: Write my speech, huh? Why? Can't I just talk?

Giniita: I know, sir, that you can talk. No one is better than you, but the secretary and her team have to write something appealing.

Cde. Mus: Yes, sir, it's their job.

Mr. Maida: Okay, okay. Let's do it then; there's no time to waste.

Giniita: Yes. They're on it at the moment.

Cde. Mus: Sure, sir.

Loud chants can be heard coming from the crowd.

Crowd: "We want Maida and his colleagues out of here!"

"Maida must go; we want this administration out!"

"Think of your nation. Stop corruption. Go home, sir."

"Join us to eradicate corruption; say no to corruption."

"Maida and his colleagues are a moral cancer in Haall."

"Shame on you all, you're destroying our homeland."

"Let's save Haallian from them!"

Mr. Maida: What's that noise outside my house? Can somebody explain to me? (*He slaps himself repeatedly, panicking.*)

Cde. Mus: It seems there are protestors outside, sir. We weren't aware of it.

Mr. Maida: Call the police and the army to deal with the situation.

Maf Zol: Sir, please leave the office and let the young generation lead. You can't win against the power of the people.

Maida: (*to Mr. Mus*) So your junior officer, Maf Zol, did this, huh?

Maf Zol: You see everyone outside there? They're prepared to die. Tell us, where are the university kids you took?

Giniita: You will regret this.

Maf Zol: No, I won't. (*Calling out loud*) Officers!

Defecting officers fill Mr. Maida's office, all pointing their guns at the leaders inside.

Maf Zol: Arrest them. Let them rot in prison for the evil they've done our people and nation.

Mr. Maida and his fellow leaders are arrested and escorted outside the office under heavy guard. The swelling crowd outside cheers as they celebrate the end of an era. Some still believe it's not the end of the corruption and nepotism, and some believe there will be a third liberation. A huge vacuum has been left with a lot of holes to fill.

The Fate Poison: The Daughter of Memories by the Lone Daughter

You can see the smile, happiness at her

birth as she entered the world;

Her beauty, intelligence, confidence,

and heart warmed everywhere.

The birds sang songs of joy as the

trees swayed from east to west;

The air was pure, and the morning

breeze was looking lovely.

Everyone—old, young, women, and

children—want to see her;

She was in love at first, her sense of

self-worth was on her face.

She has dazzling, lustrous eyes, yet

empty and sad, hope lost;

The world looks different in her eyes,

tears swelling up her eyes.

She was betrayed by the same people

who were supposed to support her;

Empty streets with children, homeless,

hopeless begging for a pound.

You can feel the shame and regret, feel

repentant about the state of affairs;

What was promised is now the dream,

team me and myself are in control.

Nothing to show the world other than the

division that has grown deeper with greed;

Haallians can do nothing, only regrets,

but they're at the point of no return.

We civilians will be on our way to the Maker

if we knew the way, and we ask why.

No clean water for decades, and we expect

politicians with clean hearts.

Where will we voice out such agony when we

don't even have freedom of expression?

Self-governance for two decades has born

no fruits. Do we need the government?

Lights fade

CPSIA information can be obtained
at www.ICGtesting.com
Printed in the USA
LVHW050400110522
718423LV00011B/834